I0724299

GODLY WARRIOR

written by A. Rorie

Copyright @2020 by Aaron Rorie

This publication contains the opinions and ideas of its author. It is intended to provide helpful and informative material on the subjects addressed in the publication. The author and publisher specifically disclaim all responsibility for any liability, loss or risk, personal or otherwise, which is incurred as a consequence, directly or indirectly, of the use and application of any of the contents of this book.

WORKBOOK PRESS LLC
187 E Warm Springs Rd,
Suite B285, Las Vegas, NV 89119, USA

Website: https://workbookpress.com/
Hotline: 1-888-818-4856
Email: admin@workbookpress.com

Ordering Information:
Quantity sales. Special discounts are available on quantity purchases by corporations, associations, and others. For details, contact the publisher at the address above.

Library of Congress Control Number: 9781607998594
ISBN-13:
                   978-1-952754-14-2 (Paperback Version)
                   978-1-952754-15-9 (Digital Version)

REV. DATE: 03 / 17 / 2020

This book is dedicated to the loving memories of Mother Joan A. Archer, Mother Gertrude D. Rorie, Elder Edward N. Rorie, Sr., Andrea Rorie, Baby Rorie, and our grandchildren.

"We are confident, I say, and willing rather to be absent from the body, and to be present with the Lord".

II Corinthians 5:8 (KJV)

ACKNOWLEDGMENTS

I would like to take this time to thank all of the people whose contributions made this book possible. First of all, I would like to thank our Lord and Savior Jesus Christ, who makes all things possible. Without you, Lord, I can do absolutely nothing. Secondly, I would like to thank my family for all of their input into this project. I would like to thank my wife Angela for taking the time to proofread this project. I would like to thank my son Aaron II and my daughter Angelica for your written ideas and comments concerning a few chapters in this book. I want to thank my daughter Alicia for proofreading and commenting about this project. I want to thank my daughter Ashley for your illustrations. Your artwork on this project is truly a blessing. I would like to thank my son Antoine for proofreading this project and lending, along with his sister Alana (also my daughter), their names to some of the characters in this book. I would like to thank Bishop Glen L. Rorie, Sr. and Mother Gertrude D. Rorie (my parents) for your financial support in getting this project off the ground. I would like to also thank District Elder Alfred and Mother Lucy Archer for your financial support towards this project. Finally, I would like to thank the entire staff at Tate Publishing Company and WorkBook Press, LLC for your guidance and suport in publishing this book. May God richly bless you all for your support and invaluable contributions to this book, with the love of Christ!

—*Deacon Aaron Rorie, Sr.*

TABLE OF CONTENTS

PLEASANT VALLEY

Once upon a time, in the small village of Pleasant Valley, there lived a God-fearing royal family whose surname was Kingsley. King Justus "The Godly Warrior" (better known as GW), Queen Justine, Prince Antoine, and Princess Alana all lived in a large castle built directly in the midst of a well-known mountain range called the Glorious Peaks. The sight of the Kingsley castle was beautiful indeed. The building was constructed mostly of stone and brick, and its balcony was skillfully carved out of pure marble. The courtyard was marked with a huge white marble cross, which had an image of a golden sword and a royal crown sculpted across the face of its cross boards.

The family usually gathered for daily Bible studies around the wooden Kingsley table in the courtyard. The table and its benches were situated carefully at the foot of the cross but just outside the front door of the castle. Resting on the table were King Justus's opened Bible, a finished glass of orange juice and a sheath for Justus Kingsley's "Sword of the Spirit." King Justus, rubbing his stomach after such a hardy breakfast, knelt down near the table to begin his daily praise and worship devotions.

While on his knees and before beginning his prayers, King Justus took one more look around the empty and strangely quiet courtyard. He could only smile as he reflected on how great God is and how richly he has blessed him and his family. The courtyard was surrounded by a strong stone wall with brick and stone towers. Even though the castle was more modern than most of the castles of its day, the courtyard still had a front entrance that was, of course, accessible by a wooden drawbridge. The drawbridge passed over a small moat that encircled the entire castle. Once outside of the castle and its courtyard walls, you would find yourself in front of a small campfire surrounded by stretches of the greenest and most well-cared-for lawn you have ever seen. It was truly one of the most beautiful days in Pleasant Valley. The view of the Glorious Peaks in the distance was just breath-taking. The skies were so sunny and blue. The cool breeze, blowing in the distance, made the day just perfect for any outdoors activity.

On this particular day, Queen Justine, Prince Antoine, and Princess Alana were away visiting the Queen's family in another village. King Justus remained behind at the castle to finish some important kingdom business. He had planned and agreed to join his family sometime during the next few days but within that particular week.

King Justus was completing his daily praise and worship devotions, when suddenly he began to sense the presence of an evil attack. The attack appeared to be coming from a well-known escaped enemy known as The Evil One (or simply E-One). King Justus immediately rose to his feet and ran over to the table where his Bible laid opened. After closing his Bible, it burst into flames and became a beautiful golden sword (the Sword of the Spirit). He placed the sword into its sheath and ran towards the drawbridge of the castle.

As he ran, his royal attire became a shiny silver suit of armor.

Fortunately, his daily Bible studies and devotions allowed him to be able to put on the *whole armor of God*. The scriptures stated that this armor would allow one to withstand the wiles of the enemy. Once he stopped at the edge of the drawbridge, a calm voice began to speak and instruct him to collect all of the blessings around the castle: Grace, Mercy, Prayer, Love, Forgiveness, etc. Only then would he be equipped to face the enemy. These blessings were shiny golden tokens that were impossible to miss. Each token was about the size of a fireplace, sculptured to resemble a particular blessing. It also had an identifying word actually written across its face. For an example Love was shaped like a heart and the word *Love* was actually written across its face. Prayer consisted of two hands placed together with the word *Prayer* written across its face. King Justus did not need a sack or a chest to collect the tokens. All he had to do was to touch the token, and it would chime as it disappeared. King Justus would then feel an overwhelming feeling of joy within his heart. The tokens were everywhere around the castle. They lay motionless on the ground, in the trees, on the hillsides, and in the moat.

The calm voice also instructed King Justus to use the Sword of the Spirit (which is the Bible or The Word of God) to blast all of the various evil temptations that E-One will send to him: Lust, Drunkenness, Murder, etc. Like the blessings, the temptations were also tokens that were impossible to miss. Each token was about the size of a blessing and was sculptured to resemble a particular temptation. For an example, Drunkenness was shaped like a wine bottle with the word *Drunkenness* written across its face. But unlike the blessings, the dull and dingy temptations appeared unannounced and attacked King Justus with a devastating force. If King Justus were ever to be struck by one of these tokens, it would send him into a painful spin that could jeopardize the success of his mission. The temptation tokens can only be defeated by using the Sword of the Spirit, which results in an explosion when contact is made. Fortunately, these tokens can't destroy King Justus as long as he has the armor and actively uses the Sword of the Spirit.

King Justus was further instructed to make his way southward across deserts, a river and through other dark territories to reach E-One's territory. There he must defeat E-One and return to his castle's courtyard before "three sevens" (which means twenty-one minutes of elapsed time). If he did not complete this task within the time allotted, the castle would be destroyed, and he would then have to do all of his first works again. After the calm voice completed giving King Justus all of the required instructions, King Justus began running around the castle grounds collecting all of the blessings that he could find. He grabbed Grace, Mercy, Prayer, Love, Forgiveness, Prosperity and the Fruits of the Spirit. He climbed a nearby mountain to find the Shield of Faith.

After King Justus returned from the mountain, he continued to prepare himself through prayer for the battle that he was about to undertake. As he began walking southward, a loud voice said, "Prepare for battle." Immediately after this announcement the temptations came. King Justus was attacked by Lust, Greed, Envy, Covetousness, Murder, Hunger, Poverty and many others. Fortunately, he remembered the instructions of the calm voice and pulled the Sword of the Spirit from its sheath. As he removed the sword from its sheath, he cried with a loud voice, "By the Word of God." The sword became the Holy Bible. As each attacked, King Justus turned and aimed his opened Bible at the oncoming temptation. Like a projectile, the Word of God shot forth from the Bible, twisting and turning as it met and destroyed each temptation with a loud explosion.

Once the last temptation was destroyed, King Justus said, "Thank you, Lord." As he lowered his Bible, which is the Sword of the Spirit, it became a sword again just before resting comfortably in its sheath. King Justus continued walking cautiously towards the south.

SUNSHINE DESERT

King Justus finally arrived at the edge of the village of Pleasant Valley. He was now confronted with crossing the vast Sunshine Desert. This desert was blanketed with several boulders (or stumbling blocks). This time, not only was King Justus facing a greater barrage of attacking temptations, but he had to avoid these stumbling blocks as well. For each time that King Justus collided with a stumbling block, he was thrown several paces backwards, losing valuable time.

As King Justus continued his southward journey, a loud voice proclaimed again, "Prepare for battle." Once again, immediately after the warning, the temptations came. The desert attack was a lot more severe than the previous attacks at Pleasant Valley. King Justus once again had to pull out the Sword of the Spirit from its sheath. As he did, he cried with a loud voice, "By the Word of God," and the sword became the Holy Bible.

Like before, as each temptation attacked, King Justus turned and aimed his opened Bible at the oncoming temptation. Once again, the Word of God

shot forth from the Bible like a projectile, twisting and turning as it met
and destroyed each of the approaching
temptations with a loud explosion. As
the last temptation was destroyed, King
Justus said, "Thank you, Lord." As he
lowered his Bible, which is the Sword of
the Spirit, it became a sword again just
before resting comfortably in its sheath.
King Justus continued his quest towards
the south. He navigated around each of
the remaining boulders (or stumbling
blocks) in a huge effort to reach the end
of the desert in a timely manner and
prepare himself for the next encounter.

GREED

PEACE RIVER

King Justus had safely completed his crossing of the desert, but now he was faced with the task of crossing a massive river called Peace River. Not only did King Justus have to cross Peace River, which separated King Justus's territory from E-One's territory, but he also had to avoid new stumbling blocks and an even greater barrage of attacking temptations. King Justus could only cross this vast river by using a nearby rowboat.

As King Justus rowed the boat and tried to avoid the stumbling blocks, he again heard a voice shout, "Prepare for battle." King Justus once again pulled the Sword of the Spirit from its sheath. As he removed the sword from its sheath, he cried with a loud voice, "By the Word of God," and the sword became the Holy Bible. Just like the previous encounters, as each temptation attacked, King Justus turned and aimed his opened Bible at the oncoming temptation. And as before, the Word of God shot forth from the Bible like a projectile, twisting and turning as it met and destroyed each of the approaching temptations with a loud explosion. Due to the difficult task of rowing, avoiding the boulders in the midst of the river, and destroying the increasing swift barrage of attacking temptations, King Justus, for the first time, suffered a few hits from the enemy that sent him into an uncontrollable spin. Once he regained control of the boat, he continued his intense battle against the temptations sent to him by E-One.

As the last temptation was destroyed, King Justus said, "Thank you, Lord" and as he lowered his Bible, which is the Sword of the Spirit, it became a sword again just before resting comfortably in its sheath. King Justus continued his southward trek. He rowed around each of the remaining stumbling blocks in a determined effort to reach the shore of

E-One's territory. Since he had allowed himself to suffer so many hits from the enemy, he had to increase his pace in rowing to make up for the time lost.

E-ONE'S TERRITORY

King Justus cautiously rowed his boat towards the shore of E-One's territory. The color of the shore's surface was a dingy pale gray and the colors in the skies were gloomy red and black. Portions of a mountain range were scattered across the gray surface in the distance. The atmosphere was very intense and also depressing.

Once King Justus stopped his rowing and rested the boat on the shore, he got out of the boat and began walking slowly towards the mountain range. King Justus again heard a voice shout, "Prepare for battle." King Justus once again pulled the Sword of the Spirit from its sheath. As he removed the sword from its sheath, he cried with a loud voice, "By the Word of God," and the sword became the Holy Bible. Just like the previous encounters, as each temptation attacked, King Justus turned and aimed his opened Bible at the oncoming temptation. And as before, the Word of God shot forth from the Bible like a projectile, twisting and turning as it met and destroyed each of the approaching temptations with a loud explosion. This time the temptations seemed to come from any and everywhere. They attacked from all directions, behind hills, from under the ground, and from the sky. King Justus found himself being hit more often than before, but he also found out the importance of putting on the whole armor as opposed to partial armor. If it weren't for this armor of protection, King Justus would most definitely have been destroyed already.

As the last temptation was destroyed, King Justus said, "Thank you, Lord." As he lowered his Bible, which is the Sword of the Spirit, it became a sword again just before resting comfortably in its sheath.

After the battle, King Justus continued walking cautiously towards the south.

THE ROAD TO E-ONE'S COLISEUM

King Justus continued his journey southward towards E-One's Coliseum. The ground had changed from a pale gray to a somewhat orange and muddy color. The area was wide open. After passing through the mountain range, there were no more mountains, trees, or any sort of plant life present. The skies were still black and red, and the atmosphere remained drenched in evil. It felt as if another attack could occur at any moment. King Justus was exhausted from the previous battles. He was hoping that the enemy would let up just enough for him to regain his strength.

Suddenly, King Justus again heard a voice shout, "Prepare for Battle." King Justus once again pulled the Sword of the Spirit from its sheath. As he removed the sword from its sheath, he cried with a loud voice, "By the Word of God," and the sword became the Holy Bible. Just like the previous encounters, as each temptation attacked, King Justus turned and aimed his opened Bible at the oncoming temptation. And as before, the Word of God shot forth from the Bible like a projectile, twisting and turning as it met and destroyed each of the approaching temptations with a loud explosion. As the last temptation was destroyed, King Justus said, "Thank you, Lord." He lowered his Bible, which is the Sword of the Spirit; it became a sword again just before resting comfortably in its sheath. King Justus continued his dangerous journey towards the south.

THE BATTLE OUTSIDE OF THE COLISEUM

A little weary from battle, King Justus continued to face more and more obstacles along the way. As King Justus continued his journey towards E-One's coliseum, he could hear that same voice proclaim, "Prepare for Battle." King Justus immediately pulled his sword from its sheath and again began shouting those faithful words, "By the Word of God." And once again, King Justus was armed with enough power to ward off and destroy every temptation that came his way.

After this battle, King Justus said, "Thank you, Lord." As he lowered his Bible, which is the Sword of the Spirit, it became a sword again just before resting comfortably in its sheath. King Justus rested awhile and took a little time to just praise God a little more for bringing him through yet another battle. Even though King Justus won the battle outside of the coliseum, he knew that the ultimate battle awaited him inside the coliseum.

King Justus was fully aware that everything was on the line concerning his family, his castle, and his village of Pleasant Valley. If he did not defeat E-One here in his territory, all would be lost. So King Justus had to stay prayed up and continue trusting God to help him in his struggles against E-One. Once again, King Justus heard that same calm voice say,

Put on the whole armor of God that ye may be able to stand against the wiles of the devil. For we wrestle not against flesh and blood, but against principalities, against powers, against the rulers of the darkness of this world, against spiritual wicked-ness in high places. Wherefore take unto you the whole armor of God that ye may be able to withstand in the evil day, and having done all, to stand. Stand therefore, having your loins girt about with truth, and having on the breastplate of righteousness; And your feet shod with the preparation of the gospel of peace; Above all, taking the shield of faith, wherewith ye shall be able to quench all the fiery darts of the wicked. And take the helmet of salvation, and the sword of the Spirit, which is the word of God: Praying always with all prayer and supplication in the Spirit, and watching thereunto with all perseverance and supplication for all saints;

Ephesians 6:11–18 (KJV)

This time, instead of the voice urging King Justus to prepare for battle, the voice quoted verses of scripture from the Word of God stressing to King Justus the need for properly putting on his spiritual armor. As King Justus thought upon these scriptures, he could hear E-One taunting and calling his name from inside of the coliseum. "King Justus! King Justus! There will be no Justus in Pleasant Valley!"

KING JUSTUS VS. E-ONE

in the Coliseum

As King Justus approached the coliseum, he could feel the atmosphere of evil intensify. He climbed the steps slowly, constantly observing his surroundings. Once again he heard a voice shout, "Prepare for battle." As King Justus stood in the far corner of the coliseum, preparing himself for the fight of his life, a snake that was coiled in the opposite corner began to grow and change into something quite hideous. It was E-One!

His head was large at the crown, and his ears were long and pointy. His face was sunken in, and he had a long forked tongue. The chains that were once used to hold him back were now broken. In his hand was a sword. E-One was determined to destroy King Justus and all that he stood for.

King Justus pulled the Sword of the Spirit from its sheath. As he removed the sword from its sheath, he cried with a loud voice, "By the Word of God" and the sword became the Holy Bible.

Just like the previous encounters, as each temptation attacked, King Justus turned and aimed his opened Bible at the oncoming temptation. And as before, the Word of God shot forth from the Bible like a projectile, twisting and turning as it met and destroyed each of the approaching temptations with a loud explosion. Temptations of Lust, Love of Money, Gambling, Murder, Poverty, etc. all were not welcome here. Unlike the other encounters, not only did King Justus shoot at the oncoming temptations, but he shot at E-One as well.

As the Word of God projectiles made contact with E-One in the opposite corner, he moaned and groaned in shear agony. King Justus continued to shoot at the temptations until the last temptation was destroyed. All that remained that needed to be defeated was E-One. King Justus knew that this was not going to be easy, but with the Lord on his side, he had already won. King Justus held the Bible tightly as he shot at E-One with everything that he had.

E-One's sword swings were beginning to get slower and weaker until finally, they ceased. As soon as E-One stopped fighting back, King Justus hit him harder with seven consecutive blows from the Word of God. E-One slumped backwards against one of the columns of the coliseum. His chains that were once broken clamped down on his wrists. The chains were also re-attached to the coliseum's columns.

"Noooo!" E-one screamed. "King Justus," he yelled "God does rule!" He knew that it was all over.

King Justus said, "Thank you, Lord." As he lowered his Bible, which is the Sword of the Spirit, it became a sword again just before resting comfortably in its sheath.

THE RETURN TO PLEASANT VALLEY

King Justus knew that he had only a short amount of time left to get back to his castle before it would be destroyed. Then suddenly he heard that familiar voice again. This time it was not shouting, "Prepare for battle." Instead it exclaimed "Well done King Justus!"

Miraculously, King Justus was no longer inside of the coliseum of E-One, but he found himself standing on the lawn just outside of his castle in Pleasant Valley. King Justus immediately ran into the castle's courtyard. The sky, which was once red and black with evil, was now light blue again. The birds were singing, and the day had been saved. King Justus knew there was only one thing left to do. He got down on his knees and began to praise God. After he finished praising and thanking God, he got on his horse and rode swiftly to meet his family. What a story he had to tell!

The images seen here are from the video game, Godly Warrior, and were used as inspiration for the book's illustrations.

www.ingramcontent.com/pod-product-compliance
Lightning Source LLC
Chambersburg PA
CBHW071842190726
48292CB00005B/1878